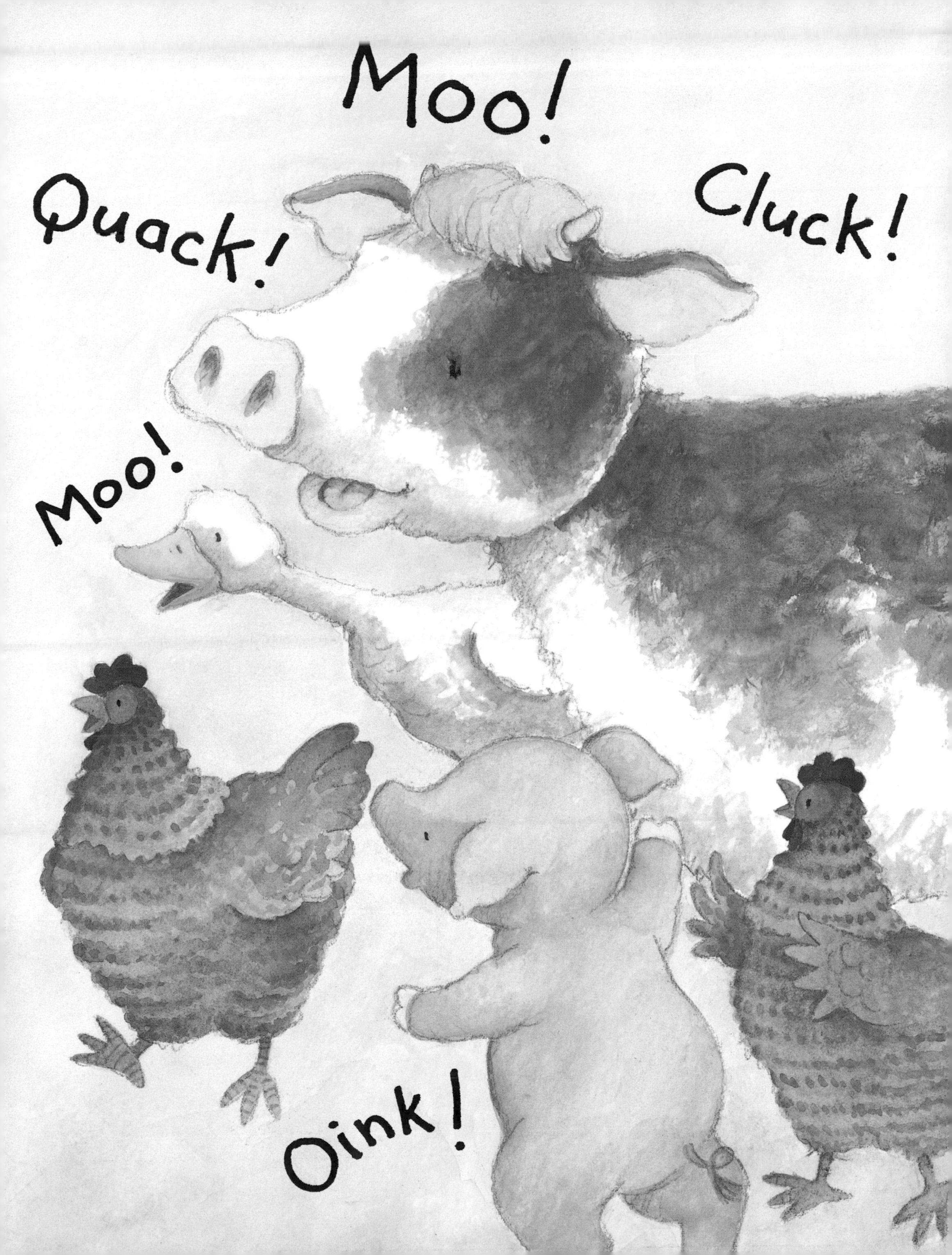
Moo!
Quack!
Cluck!
Moo!
Oink!

For Tim

First published in Great Britain in 2005
by Piccadilly Press Ltd.,
5 Castle Road, London NW1 8PR

Text and illustration copyright © Tony Maddox, 2005

Printed and bound in Belgium by Proost
Colour Reproduction by Dot Gradations Ltd, UK

ISBN: 1 85340 861 1 (paperback)
EAN: 9 781853 408618

3 5 7 9 10 8 6 4 2

A catalogue record of this book is available from the British Library

Tony Maddox lives in Worcestershire.
He has written twelve books for Piccadilly Press including
the nine Fergus titles and SPIKE'S BEST NEST.

Other Fergus titles available from Piccadilly Press:

FERGUS THE FARMYARD DOG
FERGUS'S BIG SPLASH
FERGUS'S UPSIDE-DOWN DAY
FERGUS AND MARIGOLD
FERGUS GOES QUACKERS!
FERGUS'S SCARY NIGHT
FERGUS TO THE RESCUE
FERGUS THE SEA DOG

Fergus's Secret

Tony Maddox

Piccadilly Press • London

When Farmer Bob's
tractor broke down,
the animals did their
best to help around
the farm . . .

. . . but without the tractor they found the work very tiring. After a few days the animals decided that something had to be done!

They needed to earn some money to get
the tractor repaired . . . but how?

After much discussion they came up with a plan . . .
a secret plan that Farmer Bob mustn't find out about
and that would depend on Fergus.

A few days later, the animals crept
quietly out of the farmyard leaving
Fergus behind on his own.

Shortly afterwards, Farmer Bob noticed how
quiet and empty the farmyard had become.
He decided he had better check on the animals.

He called into the barn.
"How are you today,
Mrs Cow?"

Fergus called back,
"*MOOO!*".

"Good," said Farmer Bob as he
went off to check the pigs.
Fergus had to get there
before him.
The only way was across
the muddy yard.

When Farmer Bob called across
to the pig shed, "How are
my pigs today?" a very muddy
Fergus answered, "*Oink, oink!*"

Oink
Oink!

"Good," said Farmer
Bob as he made his
way over to the hens.

Fergus managed to
reach the henhouse
just in time.

When Farmer Bob called, "How are my ladies today?"
Fergus gasped, "*Quack, quack!*" OOOPS!

"Good," said Farmer Bob as he set off towards the duck pond. Suddenly he stopped. "Hmm . . ." he puzzled, "hens don't go *quack, quack*. They go *cluck, cluck*."

Farmer Bob went back and peered through the henhouse window. He saw Fergus covered in mud, looking very sorry for himself.

"Fergus!" he cried, "What are you up to?" Fergus gave a long sigh. Now Farmer Bob would find out what the secret was.

But first Fergus needed to get cleaned up.

He led Farmer Bob to the village green.
The Summer Fair was in full swing and Farmer Bob was about to have a few surprises.

"My ducks!"
He gasped.

"My hens!"

He couldn't believe
his eyes when he saw
The World's Tallest Man.

"My pigs!" he cried.

But the biggest
surprise was yet
to come because
when he peeped
into the Fortune
Teller's tent, it
wasn't Madame
Clara he saw,
it was . . .

Madame
CLARA
See
THE
FUTURE

Mrs Cow!

There in Mrs Cow's crystal ball,
he saw his tractor, all repaired and
looking as good as new.

And guess what . . . ?

The crystal ball was absolutely right!
The animals had made enough money
to have the tractor repaired,
and everything on the farm
returned to normal.

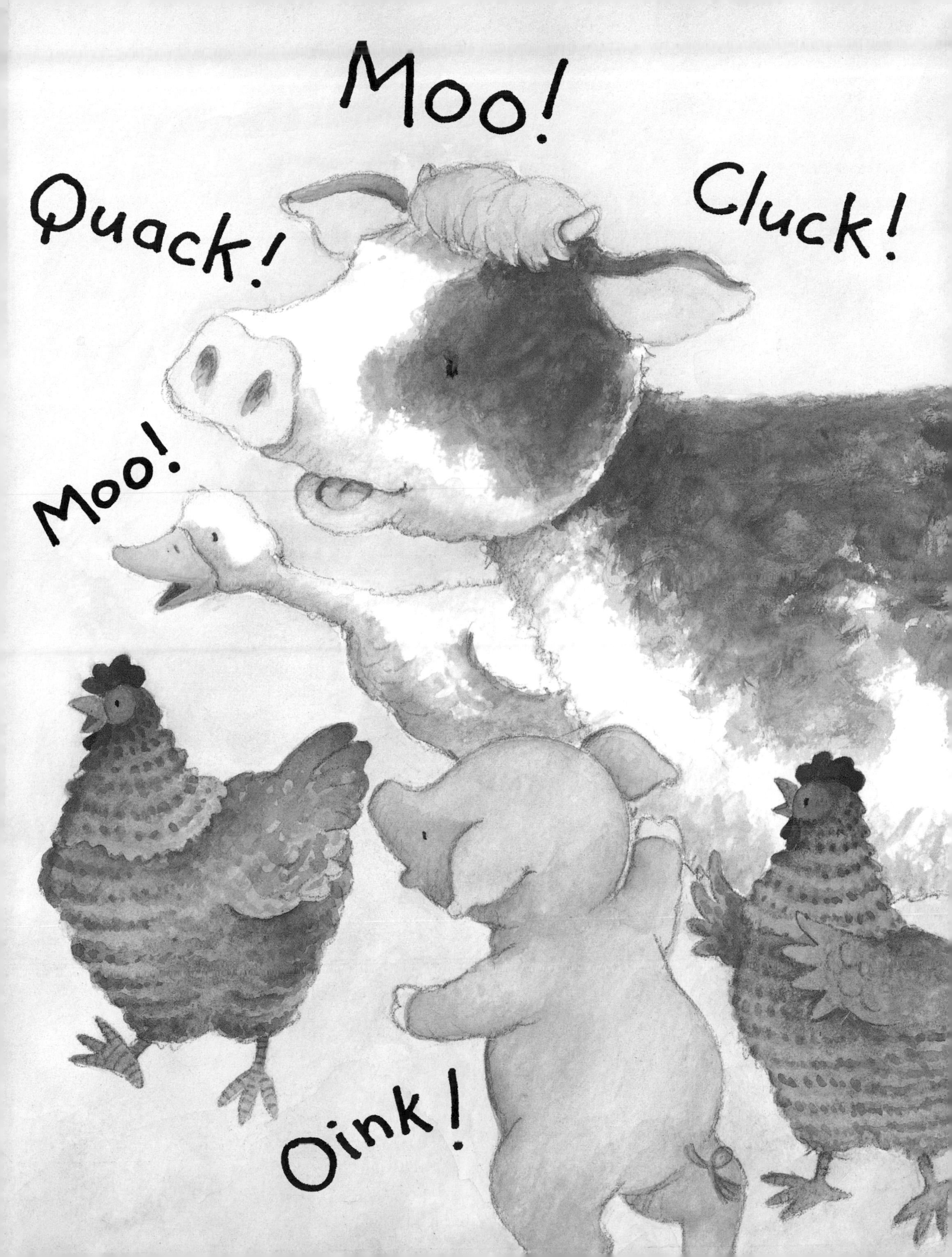
Moo!
Quack!
Cluck!
Moo!
Oink!